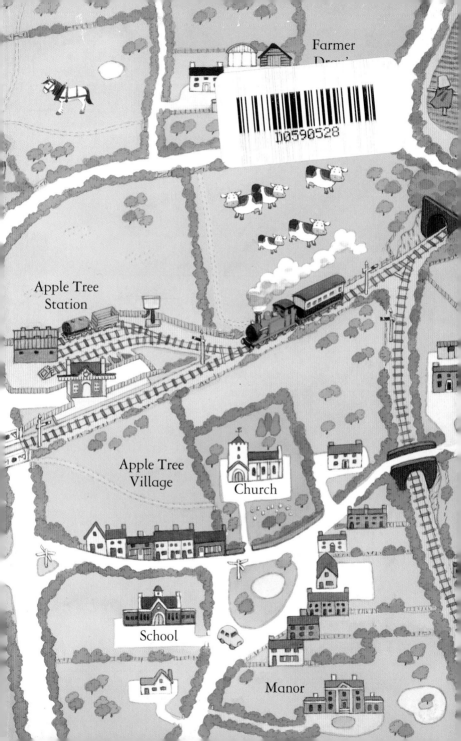

Farmer
Drav's

Apple Tree
Station

Apple Tree
Village

Church

School

Manor

Farmyard Tales

Scarecrow's Secret

Heather Amery

Adapted by Anna Milbourne

Illustrated by Stephen Cartwright

Reading consultant: Alison Kelly

Find the duck on every double page.

This story is about
Apple Tree Farm,

Mrs. Boot
the farmer,

Sam,

Poppy,

Mr. Boot,

Whiskers

and a
scarecrow.

Sam and Poppy were
helping on the farm.

They collected some eggs.

Thank you! Now can you help Daddy?

Mr. Boot was in
the barn.

"What's that?"
asked Sam.

"You'll soon see,"
said Mr. Boot.

"Please can you get
my old coat?"

They brought the coat.

"I know what it is now,"
said Sam. "A scarecrow!"

They dressed the scarecrow.

Poppy helped carry
the scarecrow outside.

Sam helped dig a hole.

They stood Mr. Straw
up in it.

"I bet he'll scare off all
the crows," said Poppy.

The next day, they
came back.

There were no birds
at all.

They looked at Farmer
Dray's scarecrow.

Birds were eating all the corn in his field.

Why was Mr. Straw
so good?

"He looks as if he's
moving," said Poppy.

"Let's go and see."

They crept across
the field.

Mr. Straw's coat was twitching.

They opened the coat
and found...

Whiskers had two
new kittens.

So that was the
scarecrow's secret!

PUZZLES

Puzzle 1

Put the pictures in the right
order to make a scarecrow.

A

B

C

D

E

Puzzle 2

What did Mr. Boot use to make the scarecrow?

coat

carrots

hat

eggs

socks

straw

What was Farmer Dray's
scarecrow made from?

coat

sticks

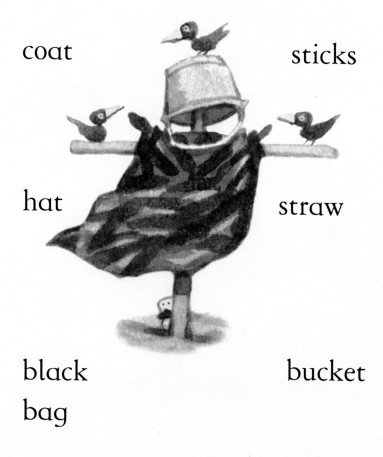

hat

straw

black
bag

bucket

Puzzle 3

Choose the right sentence for each picture.

A

They washed the scarecrow.
They dressed the scarecrow.

B

They crept across the field.
They crept across the moon.

Puzzle 4

Spot five differences between these two pictures.

Answers to puzzles

Puzzle 1

1B
2E

3C
4A

5D

Puzzle 2

hat

straw

coat

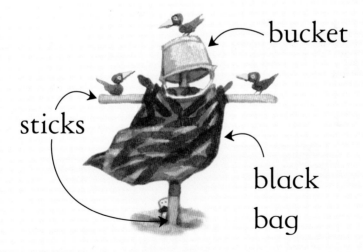

bucket

sticks

black
bag

A

They <u>dressed</u> the scarecrow.

B

They crept across the <u>field</u>.

Puzzle 4

Designed by Laura Nelson
Series editor: Lesley Sims
Series designer: Russell Punter
Digital manipulation by John Russell
and Nick Wakeford

This edition first published in 2015 by Usborne Publishing Ltd.,
Usborne House, 83-85 Saffron Hill, London EC1N 8RT, England.
www.usborne.com Copyright © 2015, 1990 Usborne Publishing Ltd.

USBORNE FIRST READING
Level Two

USBORNE FIRST READING
Farmyard Tales
Pig Gets Stuck
Illustrated by Stephen Cartwright

USBORNE FIRST READING
Farmyard Tales
The Runaway Tractor
Illustrated by Stephen Cartwright

USBORNE FIRST READING
Farmyard Tales
The Naughty Sheep
Illustrated by Stephen Cartwright

USBORNE FIRST READING
THE STONECUTTER
Retold by Lynne Benton
Illustrated by Lee Cosgrove

USBORNE FIRST READING
Old Mother Hubbard
Retold by Russell Punter
Illustrated by Fred Blunt

USBORNE FIRST READING
One, Two, Buckle My Shoe
Retold by Russell Punter
Illustrated by David Semple

USBORNE FIRST READING
There Was A Crooked Man
Retold by Russell Punter
Illustrated by David Semple

USBORNE FIRST READING
The Baobab Tree
Retold by Laura Stowell
Illustrated by Laure Fournier

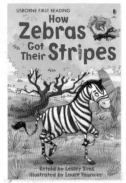

USBORNE FIRST READING
How Zebras Got Their Stripes
Retold by Lesley Sims
Illustrated by Laure Fournier